Dating Online As A Vampire

Wait What?

Abe Pritchett

A. Smith Media

CONTENTS

INTRODUCTION

It was a cold night in December, and the vampire was trying to have a normal date with a human. He had been on Tender for a while now, and he had been searching for someone who would be interested in him and his lifestyle. His life was so different from those of humans, but he wanted to find someone who could understand it.

He saw an ad that said: "I love vampires! If you're one, message me!" So he did.

The next day, they met up at an Italian restaurant. They drank wine and ate pasta as they talked about their lives and what they wanted out of them. The vampire told her about his past relationships they were good experiences for him at first, but then things started to go downhill fast. She seemed interested in what he had to say; she laughed when he made jokes about how hard it was to date other vampires because they were all so judgmental about each other's lifestyles.

CHAPTER 1: TRYING TO DATE ONLINE & TENDER WINS

After dinner, they went back to her place and made out on the couch for hours before finally going to bed together late into the night.

When he woke up the next morning.

It's not easy being a vampire.

It's not like they can just walk up to someone and ask them out. They have to be clever, and they have to be careful. If they're not careful, they can get hurt or worse.

Vampire dating is a tricky thing, but it's worth it when you find the right person.

But what if you didn't know she was human? What if you thought she was one of us? Would that make a difference? Would it change the way you feel about her? Would it change the way she feels about herself?

I think so.

The vampire had been single for a long time. He'd nearly given up hope that he would find the love of his life.

So when he saw the post on Tender, he knew it was the perfect chance to meet someone new and fall in love.

CHAPTER 2: THE TENDER DATE

But things didn't go according to plan. The human woman was rude, and she refused to go out with him even though they had matched on Tender.

The vampire left feeling defeated and lonely. But when he saw another post from a woman who looked exactly like the first one, he decided to give it another shot.

The second date was even worse than the first one! This time she spilled her drink all over him before she left him standing at the bar by himself. And then she didn't even bother texting him after that!

He was positive that he wasn't going to find his soulmate on this dating app or any other one, for that matter. But then something amazing happened: a girl messaged him! And not just any girl it was the same one who had matched with him twice before! She seemed nice enough in her message; maybe she'd be different in person than she had been online?

I had been dating Tender for a long time, and I was beginning to feel like it was time for something more. You see, I'd always been a man about town. a player, if you will but I also wanted something deeper than what Tinder could offer me.

So when I met [her name], I knew that this was my chance to settle down and find true love. She was everything I'd ever wanted: smart, beautiful, funny she had it all. And she didn't even know I was a vampire yet!

But when she found out about my secret life, things went south in a hurry. She got scared and ran away from me and our relationship as fast as she could run.

And then something incredible happened: after years of searching for her, we bumped into each other again at the grocery store! She recognized me right away and came up to talk to me about how much she'd missed me since we broke up. It turns out that she'd realized she couldn't live without me after all! We started dating again and have been inseparable ever since!

Tender was the app of choice for vampires. It was where they went to find human dates, and it was also where they went to meet other vampires.

Tender was a great place to meet people. It had all the features you would expect from a dating app: filters that let you search by age, location, and even personality traits; a messaging system that allowed users to communicate anonymously until they were ready to reveal their identities; and a rating system that ensured that the highest-rated profiles were shown first.

When I signed up for Tender, he didn't really expect much from it he just wanted to see what kind of matches he might get. After all, vampires lived forever; there wasn't much point in getting married or finding someone special if you weren't going to be around for long anyway. But then something happened: one of his matches turned out to be Veronica!

CHAPTER 3: VERONICA, HUMAN VERONICA. TENDER, ONLINE DATING GIRL, VERONICA

She was beautiful, smart, funny everything he had ever wanted in a woman but never thought he'd find. He sent her an anonymous message asking her out on a date; she replied with an anonymous message saying yes! They met at an Italian restaurant downtown and spent hours talking.

I was having a rough day. It was Friday, and I hadn't had a date in months. I couldn't even remember the last time I went on one.

So when my friend told me about Tender, a dating app for vampires, I decided to give it a try.

I downloaded it and filled out my profile: "single vampire looking for love," which seemed like an accurate description of me at the time. Then I waited for someone to message me back. And waited some more.

As the days went by, I started to lose hope that anyone would ever message me again until one day, when someone did: "Hi there! Are you free this Saturday night?" The message read. My heart leapt into my throat as I realized that someone might actually want to go out with me!

Saturday night came around quickly, and before long it was time for our date! I met my date at their house and we walked to a nearby restaurant together. We talked about our favorite books and movies as we ate dinner it was everything like any other first date would be except for one thing: My date looked like Dracula

Conclusion: Dating is hard.

I had just moved to the city and was looking for a way to meet people, so I signed up for Tender, an app that lets you find friends, love interests, or just someone to take you out on a date.

I had been on one date with another vampire when I saw his profile again. He had messaged me asking if I wanted to go out again, but I wasn't interested he was too old for my taste. But then he asked if we could be friends instead of going on any dates together.

"What do you mean?" I replied. "You're not old enough for me either."

He laughed and said: "No, silly girl! You're not old enough for me either!"

We spent hours messaging back and forth about how there were no other vampires our age in our area and how we should go out together anyway because it was fun having someone who understood us and knew what it was like to be a vampire living in the human world. We agreed that it would be fun to hang out even if we weren't dating each other.

Tender was the place to go if you were a vampire looking for a date. It was a dating app that catered specifically to vampires, and it had been around for years. But it had recently undergone a massive overhaul, and now it was more popular than ever.

The only problem was that if you were a human, it wasn't very easy to get past the first few screens without signing up as a vampire yourself. The app required that you state which kind of vampire you were and there were lots and then fill out a bunch of other questions that only vampires would know the answers to.

It wasn't difficult for me, though; I'd been dating vampires since I was in high school, so I knew all the answers. I filled out my profile quickly, entered in my contact information, and waited for someone to respond.

Pretty soon after that, my phone started buzzing with messages from interested parties. There were some pretty good-looking guys on there! And all of them seemed eager to meet up with me tonight at some bar called "Fangtasia," which sounded like fun!

So we agreed on a time and place: 8pm at Fangtasia. The guy who messaged me first said he'd be wearing

It was a dark and stormy night.

And I didn't even have to look up the weather report to know it.

I'd been on Tender for three months three long, lonely months and yet here I was again, scrolling through profiles, hoping against hope that someone would strike my fancy.

I wasn't necessarily looking for love; after all, I was only 15. But I did want someone who could make me laugh, who would understand me when no one else did, who would accept me cursed or not and my family as we were.

But every time I found someone like that, they turned out to be human. And that wasn't going to work for me.

After all, what kind of life would we have together? They'd grow old and die before their time while I stayed young forever and then what? Would we stay together forever? Or would they just sit around waiting for me until the end of time? It wouldn't be fair to them or me if that were the case!

I knew what I wanted: someone who could be with me in this world without any restrictions or limitations at all. Someone who understood how hard it was

It was a dark and stormy night.

I'd just gotten off work at the club and was ready to head home when I got a notification on Tender. It was a message from someone named [name], who had seen my profile and wanted to meet up. "Sure," I thought. "What could go wrong?"

I met Veronica at our pre-arranged location on the corner of 5th and Avenue B; we exchanged pleasantries and went for drinks at a local bar. We talked about our lives, our families, and our hopes for the future. When it came time for dinner, [name] suggested that we get some food from a nearby restaurant called The Space Station. After dinner, he drove me back over to the bar where we had met earlier that evening so we could finish our drinks and get some dessert before heading home for the night.

As soon as we walked in the door of The Space Station, I knew something wasn't right there were people everywhere! It was like rush hour at Penn Station on New Year's Evepeople bumping into each other as they pushed their way through crowds of people trying to order their food or find their tables after waiting 30 minutes.

CHAPTER 4: CONFUSION SETS IN

If this guy was a real vampire, I was doomed.

Jules, you're not going to believe this, but I met a vampire online. It's pretty crazy, and it gets even crazier from there.

I had no idea what to expect from a guy who was into dating vampires. Was he into roleplaying? Did he want someone to pretend to be a vampire? I had no clue at all.

The online dating was going well. I thought she was my soul mate, but she had one secret that made her not so perfect.

With the words "Come and get me, handsome," she gets up and leaves.

There's a long tradition of vampires living among us, undetected, who marry and raise families.

I was chatting with Betty, a vampire who lives in a graveyard.

I've been meeting a lot of vampires lately. They tell me that I should write about them.

As a veteran of many online dating sites, I was surprised by her question.

I'm a big fan of the vampire genre. I've got several favorite books about them, and I've seen more than my fair share of movies and TV shows that feature vampires. But there's one thing these concepts never seem to get quite right: vampires are supposed to be frightening, aren't they? And yet

The date went from bad to worse when we found ourselves in an argument about the existence of vampires. I mean, she actually said that vampires do not exist, and that I'm crazy for believing that they do! I was flabbergasted.

This is the first time I've sat down at my desk in weeks. I'm usually out and about, when I'm not asleep.

But then I met a girl online, who turned out to be a vampire.

I sent her a message, with the hope that she might be willing to talk about dating a vampire.

I had always imagined that dating a vampire would be just like dating any other guy. I wanted to pIf this guy was a real vampire, I was doomed.

Jules, you're not going to believe this, but I met a vampire online. It's pretty crazy, and it gets even crazier from there.

I had no idea what to expect from a guy who was into dating vampires. Was he into roleplaying? Did he want someone to pretend to be a vampire? I had no clue at all.

The online dating was going well. I thought she was my soul mate, but she had one secret that made her not so perfect.

With the words "Come and get me, handsome," she gets up and leaves.

There's a long tradition of vampires living among us, undetected, who marry and raise families.

I was chatting with Betty, a vampire who lives in a graveyard.

I've been meeting a lot of vampires lately. They tell me that I should write about them.

As a veteran of many online dating sites, I was surprised by her question.

I'm a big fan of the vampire genre. I've got several favorite books about them, and I've seen more than my fair share of movies and TV shows that feature vampires. But there's one thing these concepts never seem to get quite right: vampires are supposed to be frightening, aren't they? And yet

The date went from bad to worse when we found ourselves in an argument about the existence of vampires. I mean, she actually said that vampires do not exist, and that I'm crazy for believing that they do! I was flabbergasted.

This is the first time I've sat down at my desk in weeks. I'm usually out and about, when I'm not asleep.

But then I met a girl online, who turned out to be a vampire.

I sent her a message, with the hope that she might be willing to talk about dating a vampire.

I had always imagined that dating a vampire would be just like dating any other guy. I wanted to prove otherwise.

I spent the next few weeks talking to a vampire online. I felt myself being gradually sucked into his world, and before long I had agreed to meet him in person.

With my profile complete, I was ready to meet the man of my dreams (or so I thought).

I've spoken to many people about their experiences on dating sites. And it's one of the most frequent comments I hear: there are so many vampires out there!

I can't believe I'm saying this, but I think I've found someone who might be The One.

When I told her that I was a vampire, she didn't believe me. This had happened before.

I've been on the site for a while and most of the people I've met have been perfectly normal. But then there was this guy...

I was now getting bored, and a bit pissed off.

So, why do you look so pale?

She was delighted to meet my new friends, but when she saw their fangs, she drew back in alarm. My friends reassured her that they were only pretending to be vampires for the evening.

I was chatting with a vampire on a dating site.

Not only is she the most beautiful woman I've ever seen, she's a vampire. And on a date with me.

Not all vampires are monstrous, but this one is. I don't think I'm ready to date a vampire.

I'd been on a few dates with him, and, if he wasn't a vampire, he was at least something close to it.

I met a vampire online. He came to my apartment and drank my blood. It was pretty cool.

I had this odd experience of meeting a guy online who was a vampire. And not just some run-of-the-mill vampire but one who's been around since the 12th century.

It's been three months since I've been dating a vampire, and things are still going great.

So far, I've only met two of the challenges that I set myself. I haven't yet read any vampire fiction, or gone on a date with a real vampire... and now the time has come to confront those challenges head on.

I turned to Vampire Weekends song "Oxford Comma" for inspiration:

I talked to a lot of people, and finally found a guy that was open to being turned. I even went on a date with him, but things didn't go very well.

I'm not a vampire. I can't see in the dark and I don't have fangs. But I am immortal. And so is my girlfriend. She doesn't look it, but she can be pretty old, even by vampire standards. And you know what? She's one of the coolest people I've

She's just an ordinary girl. And he's just an ordinary guy. How can she be anything more than that, especially since he doesn't drink blood?

I've been on plenty of dates in my time, but I can't say I've ever dated a vampire.

There was only one problem: I was a vampire, and from what I could tell, she wasn't.

I'm not sure what is worse, actually, the prospect of dating a vampire or the prospect that I might be single for the rest of eternity.

I'm not one to judge, and since vampires are, by their very nature, something of a niche fetish, I wasn't necessarily surprised to find that there was a dating site for bloodsuckers out there.

I've been on plenty of dates. I've met people through friends and family. I've met them at bars, clubs, and parties. I've even met a few nerdy vampire-lovers on OKCupid. But when I received an invitation to join a secret society for vampires on Facebook, my first

I was just starting to get into the swing of things when I got a message.

I found it interesting that he called himself a vampire, but then again I had been on a lot of dates with a lot of different people and a lot of people had some pretty weird hobbies.

My friends and I were sitting in a café discussing the best way to kill an immortal enemy when my phone started buzzing. My vampire match had agreed to meet me for coffee.

Her name was Belladonna, and she was one of the most beautiful women I had ever seen.

Most of the time, I just thought he was a little strange. But that day, I felt something stirring deep inside me. It was an emotion I'd never felt before: cold, hard fear.

The questionnaire was fun to complete, and she said she'd get back to me soon, with a selection of candidates for me to choose from.

I had a great time meeting with Raul and his group, as well as seeing the sights in the city. I was relieved to find that they were just like me – mortal and not at all supernatural.

I used to date a vampire (long story), but that's a whole different story.

I was looking for some love advice at the Yahoo Answers, and I somehow ended up on a thread about dating vampires.

The reason she was glad to be herself was because she was dating a vampire.

It was a rainy afternoon recently and I was leafing through the San Francisco Chronicle's Datebook section when I saw a very interesting ad: "Dating a Vampire. San Francisco Bay Area."

I was on a quest to find someone who shared my love of horror films and good music, so I decided to join an online dating site in hopes of meeting someone special.

I can't wait to find out what happens, but only time will tell.

I hope you're not one of those people who has a problem with dating vampires. I'm not, and we're having a great time together.

I had convinced myself that it was possible. My vampire lover was going to be real.

After I signed up for the site, I did not really expect to meet anyone. But I was surprised when a few days later, I got an email from someone who had been viewing my profile.

What was I to do? I couldn't very well explain the situation to a human being without breaking the spell of the fantasy.

I am interested in getting to know you better, and I don't mean through email. If you are interested in meeting with me, please let me know.

I don't really know what to do about this, since I don't really want to hurt her feelings. I just hope she doesn't think I'm interested in more than friendship, because that would be weird.

It's a big world out there, and at least one of the dating sites I tried is full of vampires.

I've been on plenty of dates in my time, but I never thought I'd date a vampire.

She was the perfect woman for me, but there was just one little problem: she happened to be a vampire.

So I'm going to get this straight. You're an actual vampire, and you want my help in selecting a photo for your dating profile?

Actually, I've been on a lot of dates recently. And by recent, I mean that I've been going out with vampires.

She's been on the internet for 2 years. She has to be a vampire.

So, as I wrote before, here is my new profile text, written in the style of a vampire's personal ad. It's already getting a lot of attention -- but not from the kind of people I was hoping to attract.

I've never been a fan of online dating, but hell, what do I have to lose? I figure the worst that can happen is someone telling me they're disgusted by my fangs or something.

He's nineteen, and he knows that pursuing me is a bad idea, but he's going to do it anyway.

Here were two people who had every reason to be hiding their identities, and yet they were both sharing them with strangers.

The next day, I felt a little better knowing that I was unlikely to be killed by the man I met online. Though he had given me his phone number, I didn't call him.

There are also some really funny moments in the book. I've been on a few dates lately and have laughed out loud at points when watching myself through his eyes.

It is difficult to search for someone online, who is attractive and attractive. She does not want to spend the rest of her life alone, but it seems like all of the good guys are taken.

Not being able to tell if he is a vampire or not. He wants to be able to get to know someone before he tells them about his vampiric condition. He doesn't want to accidentally bite anyone!

He wants to find someone equally as awesome as himself. He struggles with finding a woman that is actually interested in him and who he can be interested in.

He can't find the right girl. He's always in a rush to find love.

After waiting for days, she still hadn't been matched with anyone. She feels like it is impossible to find a guy that appreciates her.

Jane is frustrated by the lack of quality matches on dating sites. She doesn't have time to waste, so she wants to find matches that are a good fit for her.

They are tired of always being matched with people who are not their type. They feel that they should be able to find someone who is compatible with them.

Likes to go on first dates with people that don't fully align with what she is looking for. She understands that this can be frustrating and can waste a lot of time. She has a hard time finding people that are a good fit and it is mentally exhausting.

This dating website is not always able to match you with people who share your interests. She is frustrated that no one ever seems to match her preferences. She feels like the site does not work for her and that she should be able to find a date with more ease.

The sheer number of options and difficulty in filtering through all the potential matches is exhausting. There are so many factors that can't be known until you are in person.

She isn't sure if her potential partner will text her back. She is frustrated with the time spent waiting for a response.

Her dates just don't understand the time and effort she puts into creating a great profile and maintaining a relationship. She is tired of having to always justify her choices. She wants to be respected for who she is.

Why is this all confusing?

"Huhhhhhh!" A deep breath sets in as he wakes up from a nightmare and the sun peaks in from the window.

What just happened? I was talking to her, I was her, I was him ... this does not make sense.

He looks at the ceiling confused. He quickly realized that he is in love with Veronica. This is something he never felt before.

He smiles and says, "I love her. I am in love."

BOOKS BY THIS AUTHOR

The Vampire Chronicles: New Allegiances

Josh discovers that the world is a lot of broken pieces put together, held together by a string not known for its strength but for its length. Humans, vampires, werewolves, witches, they all exist and are everywhere. All of these people look like they are humans until you take a closer look.

The adventures with his dad and friends did not end with teleporting with his mind to a place of peace, a place where witches had been hiding out for centuries. It appears witches are the most peace loving of all the groups of humans I have mentioned. Humans and vampires are the worst. They are always spoiling for a fight.

The Vampire Chronicles: Night Of Owls

A captivating adventure with vampires and humans co-mingling in everyday life. This is part of the Vampire Chronicles series.

Do Vampires Celebrate Christmas?: Of Course They Do!

It's Christmas, and we all know what that means: vampires are out and about!

Of course, not all vampires celebrate the same way. Some prefer to keep their heads down, staying in their coffins until the new year (and perhaps even longer). But others love to get into the spirit of things. They might wear a red suit or dress up as Santa Claus —though they'll be the only one who knows the true meaning of Christmas.

www.ingramcontent.com/pod-product-compliance
Lightning Source LLC
Chambersburg PA
CBHW060932130726
48001CB00006B/2533